Do Cowboys Ride Bikes?

Kathy Tucker

Illustrated by Nadine Bernard Westcott

Albert Whitman & Company
Morton Grove, Illinois

Also by Kathy Tucker and Nadine Bernard Westcott:
Do Pirates Take Baths?

Library of Congress Cataloging-in-Publication Data

Tucker, Kathy.
Do cowboys ride bikes? / written by Kathy Tucker; illustrated by Nadine Westcott.
p. cm.
Summary: Humorous rhyming answers to fourteen questions
about what it's like to be a cowboy.
ISBN 0-8075-1693-7
[1. Cowboys—Fiction. 2. Stories in rhyme.]
I. Westcott, Nadine Bernard, ill. II. Title.
PZ8.3.T793Df 1996
[E]—dc20 95-52650
CIP AC

Design by Scott Piehl.
Text set in Goudy Sans & Giddy Up.
Art rendered in ink and acrylics.

For my father, who lives in the West
and doesn't like to stay inside.
K. T.

For Sarah and her pony, Chocolate.
N. B. W.

Where do cowboys live?

They live in the West,
way out on the range,
where there isn't even a town;
where nobody tells them
to stay inside
or to keep their voices down.

What does a cowboy look like?

You know by his outfit:
his jeans and his chaps,
a Stetson that keeps off the heat.
He wears a bandana
(for blood, sweat, and tears)
and good leather boots on his feet.

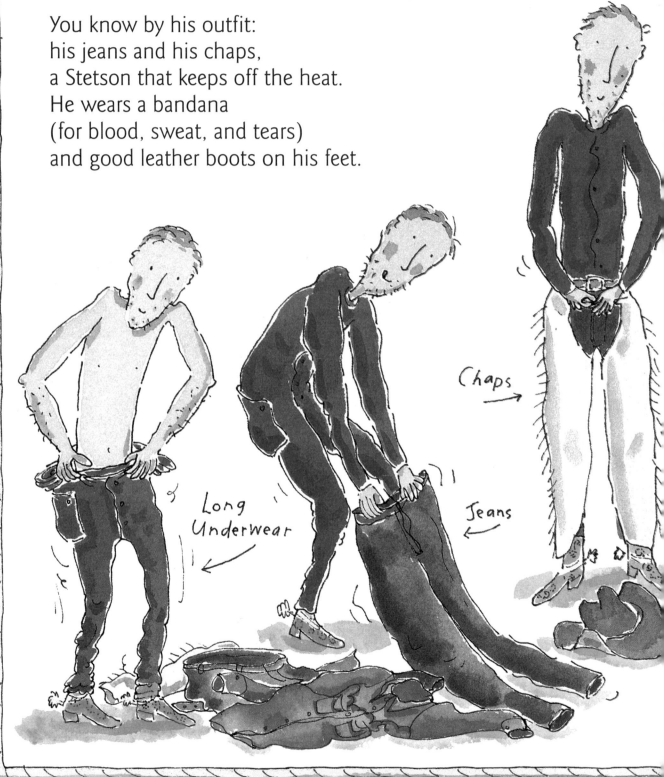

Long
Underwear

Jeans

Chaps

Stetson

Bandana

Boots

Do cowboys ride bikes?

They don't have much time
for riding their bikes
'cause a cowboy must stay with his horse.
He rides it all day,
gives it plenty of hay,
and lots of cool water, of course.

What does a cowboy need?

He needs a good rope
to twirl in the air,
and a bedroll for sleeping at night;
some silvery spurs
that jingle and clink,
and a saddle that feels just right.

What do cowboys eat?

It's biscuits for breakfast
with coffee that's black
as a mud puddle deep in the night.
For supper it's bacon
and beans, beans—BURP!
(Not a scoop of ice cream in sight.)

How do cowboys talk?

A calf is a *dogie*,
food is called *grub*,
at bedtime the boys *hit the hay*.
They call, "Howdy partner!
Let's mosey along,"
and they shout, "Ti yippee ti yay!"

What do cowboys do in the spring?

They have a big round-up,
to look for the strays
who've roamed all over the land.
They find the new calves,
rope 'em and brand 'em,
and count 'em, five on each hand.

What happens after the round-up?

They drive all the cattle
along an old trail
to a town where they will be bought.
It's a mighty hard trip,
but a cowboy is tough,
though he's dusty and tired and hot.

Are there dangers on the trail?

There always are dangers
like rustlers and crooks
called Snake-Head and Itchy Dan.
When no one's looking,
they sneak up and steal
as many cows as they can.

Do cowboys catch the rustlers?

Of course they catch
the lousy varmints—
they leave a messy trail.
While the rustlers snooze,
the cowboys pounce!
and haul 'em off to jail.

What's a stampede?

Sometimes the cattle
just start to run
if they're scared by a storm or a shout.
The cowboys must chase 'em
into a circle
till everyone's plum tuckered out.

What do cowboys do in town?

They take a hot bath,
slick down their hair,
and put on their very best duds.
They dance with the gals,
play horseshoes and chess,
and slug down some root beer with suds.

Do cowboys ever take their boots off?

They don't take them off,
not even to sleep
(though their mothers have tried and tried),
for they have to be ready
when trouble comes
to leap in the saddle and ride.

What do cowboys do at night?

They use some sagebrush
to clean their teeth,
and they build the campfire high.
Then they croon sweet songs
to quiet the cows
while the moon shines in the sky.

Good night!